"For, lo, the winter is past,
the rain is over and gone;
The flowers appear on the earth;
the time of the singing of birds is come."

—SONG OF SOLOMON 2:11, 12.

Thank You, God, for Spring

By Jane Belk Moncure
Illustrated by Frances Hook

THE CHILD'S WORLD
ELGIN, ILLINOIS 60120

Library of Congress Cataloging in Publication Data

Moncure, Jane Belk.
  Thank you, God, for spring.

  (The Four seasons)
  Published in 1975 under title: Spring is here!
  SUMMARY: Describes in verse the sights, smells,
sounds, and activities of spring.
  [1. Spring—Fiction. 2. Stories in rhyme]
  I. Hook, Frances. II. Title. III. Series.
PZ8.3.M72Tj 1979   [E]   79-10031
ISBN 0-89565-079-7

Distributed by Standard Publishing, 8121 Hamilton Avenue,
Cincinnati, Ohio 45231.

PICTURE WORDS

a kite

baby robins

a baseball

a bat

rain

carrots

flowers

baby ducks

a frog

a turtle

a pond

radishes

bunnies

cucumbers

I will sing on this warm spring day.

Winter's cold has gone away.

I will get my baseball and my bat.

Forget my coat and my winter hat.

I will stay outside and play.

Thank You, God, for a warm spring day.

Thank You, God,
for the birds that sing
in spring,
for the baby robins
that chirp and cry
as I walk by.

Thank You, God, for the things that grow
after the sunshine melts the snow.

All through the winter, no one could tell
that lilacs have a special smell.
I will take my mother a spring surprise
and make her smell and close her eyes.

In spring, God's world is full of things,
things that wiggle, hop, and sing,
things that crawl in the tall green grass.

Where are you going so fast, Mr. Turtle?
Where are you going so fast?

Thank You, God, for warm spring rain
that sprinkles every bush and tree
and splashes raindrops over me!

Thank You, God, for a windy day,
for the chance to fly
my kite up high,
and watch it sail away.

Thank You, God,
for all the
wonderful things
spring brings:
for the birds,

and the
flowers,

for turtles

and frogs,

for ducklings
and slippery
polliwogs,

for the
fluffy brown
bunnies
who like to play

hide and seek

on a

warm

spring

day.

21

Soon the seeds
in my garden will
sprout and grow

into carrots
and radishes
and cucumbers.

So,
thank You, God,
for everything
in the wonderful,
sunshiny season
of spring.

Thank You, God, For Spring

J.B.M.

Jane Belk Moncure

Take a walk in spring and sing a hap-py song. Look up look down, look all a-round as you skip a-long. Oh! Whis-tle to the rob-in. Can you hear him sing? Is-n't it a love-ly thing to go a-walk-ing in the spring? Thank You, God, for spring.